Oliver Twist

Retold from the Charles Dickens
original by Kathleen Olmstead

Illustrated by Dan Andreasen

Sterling Publishing Co., Inc.
New York

Library of Congress Cataloging-in-Publication Data

Olmstead, Kathleen.
Oliver Twist / retold from the Charles Dickens original ; abridged by Kathleen Olmstead ; illustrated by Dan Andreasen ; afterword by Arthur Pober.
p. cm.—(Classic starts)
Summary: An abridged version of the adventures of the orphan boy who is forced to practice thievery and live a life of crime in nineteenth-century London.
ISBN 1-4027-2665-1
[1. Orphans—Fiction. 2. Robbers and outlaws—Fiction. 3. London (England)—Fiction. 4. Great Britain—History—19th century—Fiction.]
I. Andreasen, Dan, ill. II. Dickens, Charles, 1812–1870. Oliver Twist.
III. Title. IV. Series.

PZ7.O515Oli 2006
[Fic]—dc22

2005015840

2 4 6 8 10 9 7 5 3 1

Published by Sterling Publishing Co., Inc.
387 Park Avenue South, New York, NY 10016

Distributed in Canada by Sterling Publishing
c/o Canadian Manda Group, 165 Dufferin Street
Toronto, Ontario, Canada M6K 3H6
Distributed in Great Britain and Europe by Chris Lloyd at Orca Book Services, Stanley House, Fleets Lane, Poole BH15 3AJ, England
Distributed in Australia by Capricorn Link (Australia) Pty. Ltd.
P.O. Box 704, Windsor, NSW 2756, Australia

Printed in China

Designed by Renato Stanisic

Sterling ISBN 1-4027-2665-1

Contents

CHAPTER 1

Oliver Twist

Regrettably, our story must begin on a note of sadness. It is an unfortunate truth that not all beginnings are happy ones. This particular story opens in a workhouse. There was a time—the same time that our story takes place—when too many cities and towns were home to these large, cold buildings. Men who could not pay their bills were sentenced to hard labor here. Women and children with no place else to go lived and worked here. Children left on doorsteps with no family to call their own spent their days in the bottle-washing factories. There is nothing beautiful or warm one can say about a workhouse. Only that this is where our young hero, Oliver Twist, came into the world.

In fact, there was almost no story to tell at all. For the first few moments of his life, Oliver did not take to breathing right away. Now, things might have been different had he been surrounded by loving aunts and grandmothers. They would have fussed and worried over him. Unfortunately, there was only the doctor, who quickly turned back to the fire, and an old woman who sat with Oliver and his mother. So, it was up to the baby to fight it out on his own. And fight he did. After a few sniffs, some struggling coughs, and a sneeze he let out a long—and quite strong—wail.

The blanket on the bed rustled as Oliver's mother moved. She slowly raised her pale face from the pillow and said quietly, "Let me see the child before I die."

The doctor looked back from the fire. "Oh, you must not talk about dying yet," he said.

"I should say not!" the old woman added. "When she has lived as long as I have then she can talk about dying. I've brought thirteen children into this world and watched all but two die. I know a thing or two about living and dying. She has no reason to talk like that."

The patient shook her head. She stretched her hand toward the child. The doctor placed Oliver in her arms. She pressed her cold white lips onto the baby's forehead. It was a tender, loving kiss. This was a special moment between mother and son. She then passed her hand over her own face. Her head dropped onto the pillow and she was dead. The doctor and old woman worked to save her. They pounded on her chest and rubbed her hands, but there was no use. She was gone.

"Oh, the poor dear," the old woman cried. "How sad for the little one." She picked Oliver up. He lay quietly in her arms.

"Well, there's nothing more I can do," the doctor said. He put his hat on and picked up his bag. "If the child cries, you can give him some gruel."

He stopped before heading out the door. "Shame, too. She was a pretty young thing. Do you have any idea who she was or where she came from?"

"None, sir," the old woman replied. "She arrived last night during that terrible rain. No shoes, no bags. She was very sick and ready to give birth."

The doctor walked back to the bed. He raised the young woman's left hand. "The same old story," he said, shaking his head. "I see there's no wedding ring. Ah, well! Good night," he said and quickly walked out the door.

The old woman sat before the fire and wrapped the infant in a blanket. She told the woman who ran the workhouse, Mrs. Bumble, that a baby boy had been born.

"Ach," Mrs. Bumble said. "Another orphan for the workhouse to take care of." She looked at the baby with disgust. "Another mouth to feed. More money from my small allowance."

There was nothing to envy in the life of an orphan. Especially an orphan raised in the workhouse. Their lives were filled with hard work, little play, and very little food. Very few showed pity or kindness toward them, especially those people who took care of them.

Mr. Bumble, the husband of the woman who ran the workhouse, was a town official. The workhouse was one of his responsibilities. He made sure that everything was to the liking of the town council and workhouse board. He was a man who liked to use his power, but failed to realize that no one feared him. His wife, in particular, thought him foolish. The Bumbles looked like one another. Both were short, round, and mean-spirited.

It was Mr. Bumble who gave Oliver his last name. He used the alphabet to keep track of all the new orphan names. When the last orphan came to them, Bumble was at the letter S. Therefore, Bumble gave him the name Swubble. As T was next in line, this baby was named Twist. The orphan after Oliver received the name Unwith, and the one after that Vilkins.

"Very good, Mr. Bumble," Mrs. Bumble said. She wrote Oliver's name in the registry book. "It's official now."

"All a part of the job, Mrs. Bumble," Mr. Bumble answered. "A town official's job is rarely done." Mr. Bumble did not notice his wife rolling her eyes at his comment. He was too distracted by the screaming baby beside him.

Oliver cried loudly. If he could have known that he was an orphan, left to the not-so-tender mercies of church-wardens and the workhouse staff, perhaps he would have cried all the louder.

CHAPTER 2

Life in a Workhouse

Despite the many obstacles before him, Oliver Twist survived. He was now ten years old and still in the workhouse. His days were filled with too much work and far too little food.

Mrs. Bumble was given a weekly allowance from the town council to feed and dress her charges. She was a very careful woman and was always worried about money. Unfortunately, she was more worried about her personal income than the well-being of the children in her care.

Therefore, she kept the majority of the allowance for herself and used the rest to feed the children. In order to make the supply of gruel go farther, Mrs. Bumble watered it down.

Even though this meal of thin porridge was not enough to meet the needs of a growing boy, Oliver did grow. He was a small, thin boy with pale blonde hair, but he reached his tenth birthday without too much trouble. His best friend Dick had a much tougher time. Dick was very weak and often sick. Oliver had to help him with his work washing bottles in the factory. In fact, he was so worried about Dick that he sometimes tried to pass him the last bits of gruel in his bowl. His friend always refused.

"No, Oliver," Dick said. "You have too little to spare."

"But maybe you'll feel better with more food," Oliver replied.

"A few tiny drops of gruel won't do me much good," Dick said. "We all need more than that."

The room where the boys were fed was a long stone hall. A copper pot stood at one end. The boys walked to the front in a single-file line. They held their wooden bowls up and Mr. Bumble dropped a ladleful of gruel in.

The boys sat down at the long tables that filled the hall. They had to wait until everyone was seated. Anyone caught sneaking a bite was punished. The boys held their spoons while bowing their heads for grace. As soon as the signal was given, the boys dug in to their meals. They were done in a matter of seconds. The boys' bowls never needed washing. They polished them with their spoons until they shone again.

On the night that Oliver's life changed forever, a new boy was sitting at his table. His father was a butcher who could not pay his bills and lost his shop. This new boy was not used to the great hunger of the workhouse. He did not understand that the council had no wish to change. This new boy had a plan.

"One of us needs to talk to Mr. Bumble," he said. "We've got to ask for something more to eat."

The other boys agreed that action was needed. The new boy held several pieces of straw in one hand. All the boys at the table—except Dick—took turns picking one. Oliver won the contest by drawing the longest straw. All the boys slapped him on the back. Dick, however, looked worried. He thought this might be a bad idea.

As soon as everyone was finished eating—for it did not take long—Oliver rose from the table. He walked down the long row toward Mr. Bumble and the copper pot of gruel.

Poor Oliver was shaking

with fear. He held his bowl toward Mr. Bumble and quietly said, "Please sir, I want some more."

The hall was silent. All of the boys in the long hall watched Oliver in shock. Everyone waited for Mr. Bumble's response. At first he looked confused by this small boy. It seemed impossible that someone would ask for something else. The Bumbles and the workhouse board believed they were very generous people. They thought these boys and the other workhouse inmates should be grateful for the little they received. As he slowly realized that Oliver was holding up an empty bowl, Mr. Bumble became angry.

"What??!" Mr. Bumble screamed.

"Please, sir." Oliver tried to speak more clearly. He tried to sound more forceful and brave. "I want some more."

"More??!" Mr. Bumble yelled. "More??" He was furious! How dare this ungrateful boy ask for more! It was impossible to believe any child could have such nerve and greed.

"Grab him," Bumble shouted. Two members of the workhouse staff grabbed Oliver by his arms. They carried him from the long hall and locked him in a tiny room.

CHAPTER 3

A New Home

Mr. Bumble went into a back room where the board was having its supper. There was, of course, no gruel in sight at this meal. The board members were dining on roast chicken and roast beef with potatoes, gravy, turnips, and peas. No less than four pies were waiting for them on a side table for dessert. Both the table and the men were filled with rich and delicious food.

"I am sorry to deliver bad news," Mr. Bumble said. He was out of breath from running. "But Oliver Twist, one of our young charges, has gone mad." Mr. Bumble told the board members the events that happened only minutes ago. They reacted as one might expect, with shock and horror.

"Impossible," said a man in a white vest. "Such an ungrateful child does not deserve the comforts of this establishment."

The other board members agreed. They banged on the table and said, "Here, here" and "Aye, aye."

"I fear that he will only cause more trouble," Mr. Bumble said. "It would do us no good if he convinced other boys to do the same."

"Very well then," said the man in the white vest. "Post a sign, Mr. Bumble. Offer this boy and a reward of five pounds to anyone who will take him." The board members once again pounded on the table in agreement. Mr. Bumble went to do as he was told.

The sign was up for several days before Mr. Sowerberry, the local undertaker, came to the workhouse. He was there on business when he noticed the sign. He was happy to take the five pounds, but he was not so sure about the boy. Mr. Bumble took him straight to the board to discuss Oliver's fate.

"Who's to know if the boy will work hard?" Mr. Sowerberry asked. "What good will it do me if I don't get enough work from him? What if it takes too much food and I get too little work in return?"

"We've been careful to feed the boy very little," Bumble said. "So he doesn't demand much." Bumble was careful to avoid mentioning the incident in the long hall.

"We'll allow a trial period," the man in the white vest said. "If Oliver is to your liking, you will train him as an undertaker's assistant. If he does not agree with you, you may bring him back."

"And I keep the five pounds, of course," said the undertaker.

The man in the white vest cleared his throat. "Of course," he said slowly. "Whatever suits you best, Mr. Sowerberry. We do ask, though, that you take the boy right away. We'll be happy to be rid of him. One less boy to feed and all that."

So Oliver Twist was given a small bundle of shirts and a wool blanket. They rushed him out the door with the undertaker. He did not even have time to say good-bye to Dick. Mr. Sowerberry led him away from the workhouse through gently falling snow.

For the first time in his ten years, Oliver was away from the Bumbles and the workhouse. It was all very frightening, but Oliver felt some excitement, too. He hoped he was on an adventure. He felt certain, however, that no matter what happened, his new life had to be better than the old one.

CHAPTER 4

A Bit of Meat

It was already evening when Oliver and his new master arrived at the undertaker's home. Mr. Sowerberry entered the front hall and lit a small candle. Oliver stepped in slowly. He stood quietly by the door, waiting for his eyes to adjust to the gloomy hall.

"Mrs. Sowerberry," Mr. Sowerberry called. "Would you come here for a moment?"

Mrs. Sowerberry appeared from a back room. She was a small, thin woman who looked like she never smiled. She placed her hands on her hips and said, "Well?" She did not sound very happy.

"My dear," said Mr. Sowerberry. "I've brought home a workhouse boy. We can put him to work in the shop."

"He looks pretty small," she frowned.

"Well, yes," Mr. Sowerberry said. "He is rather small. I'm sure that he will grow, though."

"Of course," she snapped. "And on our food and money. These workhouse boys always cost more than they're worth."

Mrs. Sowerberry took Oliver by the shoulders. She turned him around, checking his hair and teeth. Oliver did as she asked. He showed her his hands and tried to answer her questions. But every time he started to say something, his eyes welled up with tears. No words would come out.

"Very well then," Mrs. Sowerberry sighed. Her husband had too many plans, she thought. They would never get ahead at this rate. Not if he continued to bring home strays. "Come down to the cellar. Charlotte will give you some meat."

Oliver's eyes grew wide at that word. Meat! Could it really be true? Was he about to enjoy meat for dinner? The boy's mouth started to water.

Mrs. Sowerberry pulled him by the arm. She dragged him down the cellar stairs and pushed him toward the fire. He startled a young woman standing by the fire. Charlotte almost dropped her spoon into the cooking pot. She looked surprised and confused by this pale, thin boy.

"Charlotte," Mrs. Sowerberry said. "My husband has brought home another boy. This one's from the workhouse." Mrs. Sowerberry started cleaning up Charlotte's work area. It was obvious that Mrs. Sowerberry liked things done her own way. "Give him whatever scraps you have. There must be something you were saving for the dog."

Oliver ate his supper quickly. He pulled the meat from the bone, chewed off the extra bits of fat, and sucked out the last of the flavor. Charlotte and Mrs. Sowerberry watched with horror. They had never seen anything like it. Oliver knew he should be more careful about his manners, but he could not stop. Although his dinner was small by most standards, it was the largest he had ever enjoyed.

When he was done Mrs. Sowerberry said, "Grab your things, boy. We'll make up your bed in the front room. You don't mind sleeping among the coffins, do you?" She did not wait for an answer. Once again she dragged him by the arm. "Don't suppose it matters much if you do mind, though. There's no place else for you to go."

Oliver found himself in a room full of coffins. Some were set up on platforms for display. The lids were open, revealing plain or satin interiors. Many more were leaning up against the walls. Mrs. Sowerberry handed him a small candle. She told him not to waste it, as he was not likely to get another.

"Thank you, Ma'am," he said meekly. "I'll be careful."

"My word!" she exclaimed. "It does speak!" For a second, Oliver thought she might smile. He was wrong. "Now get to sleep, boy. We wake up early here and there'll be no dawdling." Mrs. Sowerberry left Oliver all alone. She shut the door tightly and walked away.

Oliver was scared, but only because things were new. He had no idea what to expect. He was so used to the routine of the workhouse that he could not imagine another way of living. Oliver was to learn a new trade in the morning. He would soon be an undertaker's assistant. He promised himself that he would work hard and not disappoint anyone.

Oliver blew out the candle. He lay on his mat thinking about his mother. He wondered what his life might have been like had she lived. Oliver thought about his mother almost every night.

Whenever the room full of workhouse boys settled down and everything was dark and quiet, he wondered what she looked like. Did she have the same hair color? Did she have a soft voice? He knew nothing about her, but he missed her terribly. Somehow he knew that she would have been tender and kind. He knew that she would have loved him dearly. She would have kissed him on the forehead every night and helped him say his prayers. Oliver fell asleep in his new home with a very heavy heart.

CHAPTER 5

Noah

Oliver woke up in the morning to the sound of kicking at the door. He got up quickly and opened the door. An angry young man stood in the hallway.

"I take it you're the new workhouse boy," he said.

"Yes," Oliver replied. "My name is Oliver Twist." He tried to appear friendly. Although this was not a promising start, this young man might be a new friend.

"I'm Noah Claypole." Noah poked Oliver in

the chest as he spoke. "I've been here a long time. Don't forget that I'm in charge of you." The young man stared at Oliver. "How old are you?"

"I'm ten years old," Oliver said quietly. The promise of a new friend was quickly fading. Oliver knew that Noah was looking for trouble.

"Huh," Noah said. "Pretty small for ten."

"Noah! Oliver!" Mrs. Sowerberry called from the cellar. "Come and get your breakfast."

Charlotte handed each of the boys a plate. "You didn't waste any good bits on the work-house boy, did you?" Noah asked. He put his arm around Charlotte's shoulders.

"Of course not, Noah," she giggled. "I only gave Oliver the fatty bits of meat."

"You see how it is, Oliver?" Noah asked. "You'll get nothing special here. You won't take my place as the undertaker's assistant."

Oliver knew that Noah spoke the truth. He knew it would be difficult working with a bully.

No one was on Oliver's side. Noah picked on him. Charlotte favored Noah. Mrs. Sowerberry yelled at everyone. Mr. Sowerberry paid almost no attention to anyone. This was to be the pattern of Oliver's days. He worked hard, ate fatty bits of meat, tried to avoid Noah, and wished for a friend.

Many weeks passed with little change. Oliver helped Mr. Sowerberry as best he could. Every night he slept in his room with the coffins, thinking about his lost mother. Every morning he woke up to Noah's taunts and a fatty piece of meat.

One morning Noah was in a particularly bad mood. Both the undertaker and his wife had yelled at him that morning. He had been caught taking a nap and then spending too much time talking to Charlotte. Noah decided to take it out on Oliver.

"So, Workhouse," he said to Oliver. Noah often called Oliver by that name. "How's your mother?"

Normally Oliver would take Noah's abuse without a word. This was not to be one of those times. "My mother is dead," Oliver said sternly. "Leave her out of it." His face grew red with anger.

"Ah, well," Noah smiled. "She's better off."

"Take that back!" Oliver said. He stood up and clenched his fists.

Noah laughed. "We're all better off. Don't need one more person living off the workhouse."

"What did you say?" Oliver's eyes were filled with tears. This was the first time Oliver had ever felt real anger. Through all of the unfairness Oliver had been forced to live with, no one had ever insulted his mother.

"You heard me," Noah replied. "We're all better off."

Oliver jumped on top of Noah and began hitting him. Noah dropped to the floor and cried out for help. Mrs. Sowerberry and Charlotte arrived in a few moments. They pulled Oliver off Noah.

Despite his small body, it was hard to pull Oliver back.

"What on earth happened?" asked Mrs. Sowerberry.

"I don't know, Missus," Noah lied. He sat up and rubbed his head. Noah was confused. He never thought Oliver would fight back. "He suddenly went mad," Noah said.

They could not calm Oliver down. He tried to get out of their grasp. As a last resort, they threw Oliver into a coffin and Mrs. Sowerberry sat on top of it. "Noah," she said. "Run and get Mr. Bumble. And hurry before this boy knocks me clear off."

CHAPTER 6

The Escape

Mr. Bumble and Noah returned a half hour later. Mrs. Sowerberry and Charlotte were stressed and worried. Oliver was still banging on the coffin lid. He demanded to be let out. He was not the quiet, shy boy who had arrived a month earlier.

"You're having some trouble, I see," said Mr. Bumble.

"Of the worst kind," said Mrs. Sowerberry. "Your workhouse boy has gone mad."

Mr. Bumble tried to calm Oliver down, but the boy would not listen. "Aren't you afraid of me, Oliver?" he asked. Mr. Bumble used his loudest voice. He puffed his chest out and yelled the words.

"No!" Oliver called from inside the coffin.

Mr. Bumble was shocked. "Well, Madam," he said to Mrs. Sowerberry. "I see what the problem is. It's meat."

"Excuse me?" she asked surprised. "Why would that be a problem?"

"Meat, Madam, meat," Mr. Bumble repeated himself. "You've overfed him. You've raised a spirit in him."

Mr. Bumble and Mrs. Sowerberry continued to discuss the problems with meat until Mr. Sowerberry returned. He was shocked to hear about Oliver. Mr. Sowerberry had thought the boy showed promise. He was certainly more reliable than Noah. There was no arguing with the facts, though. His wife, Charlotte, and Noah all said Oliver had suddenly gone mad without cause. It was decided the boy would return to the workhouse in the morning.

"Noah," Mr. Sowerberry said sadly. "Lock Oliver in the cellar. We'll deal with this tomorrow."

Noah was only too happy to help out. He pushed Oliver toward the cellar. The young orphan boy ran quickly down the stairs. Mrs. Sowerberry threw Oliver's few things after him and locked the door. Noah tried not to smile too much as he passed the others.

Oliver sat at the bottom of the stairs wondering what he should do next. Soon it would be dark and he had no candle. He thought about the workhouse. He missed his friends, especially Dick, but Oliver could not bear the thought of going back.

"The thing to do," Oliver said to himself, "is

to run off and make my fortune." Oliver knew he must head to London. London was a city filled with opportunities. He was sure to be a success.

Oliver waited until the first light of dawn. He stacked some crates beneath a window, climbed on top, and pushed the window open. Taking hold of his small bundle, Oliver climbed out into the street and turned toward the main road. Mr. Sowerberry often took him through town on errands, so Oliver knew the way. Except for a few vegetable sellers setting up their stalls, there was almost no one on the street. Oliver looked at the road signs. He followed the one that pointed to London.

CHAPTER 7

Saying Good-bye

Oliver made a short stop on his way to London and his fortune. He stopped by the workhouse first. It was just after dawn and some boys were already walking in the yard. Oliver knew that Dick would be among them. Oliver waited by the fence until he spotted his friend. He called softly and waved. Luckily, Dick noticed him and walked over.

"Oliver!" Dick said. "What on earth are you doing here? I thought they took you away forever!"

"You must tell no one that you've seen me," Oliver said. "I've run away from the undertaker's. I'm off to London to make my fortune."

"But London is so far, Oliver. How will you make it?" Dick started to cough. He held onto the fence for support.

"How pale you are!" Oliver said. He was very worried about his friend. "You should go see the doctor this very morning."

Dick shook his head. "He's been to see me. He says there's no use. He says I'm quite sick and there isn't much he can do. I'll just have to wait it out." Dick saw how much this upset Oliver. "Don't worry about me," he said. "I'll be fine no matter what. Just take care of yourself. And remember that you're the finest friend anyone could ask for." Dick reached through the bars of the fence to hug Oliver. "Good-bye, Oliver! God bless you!"

This was the first blessing that Oliver had ever

known. Throughout all the struggles and sufferings and troubles that Oliver was soon to face, he never forgot it.

Oliver went back to the main road and started his long journey. His shoes were in bad shape. They were a few sizes too big. The bottoms were about to fall off. The laces were worn. His feet hurt but he kept walking. He saw several carts and buggies along the way, but none would stop for him. So Oliver continued to walk. It seemed like he would have to walk all the way to London. He stopped at a farmhouse to beg for food. A woman gave him some bread and butter. At night he slept in a field, covering himself with his blanket. He woke up the next day at dawn and started walking again. Oliver had four days of endless walking, begging for food at farmhouses and sleeping in fields. On the morning of the fifth day, he saw the city of London in the distance. At long last he was lucky enough to get a ride with a farmer heading into market. Oliver sat in the back of the cart with the baskets of vegetables. At least he would arrive in his new city in style.

CHAPTER 8

London at Last

Oliver could not believe his eyes when they entered the city. There were so many people! So much activity! He could not decide which way to look first. There were tall buildings everywhere with black smoke pouring out of chimneys. Men and women shouted to each other and passersby as they tried to sell their goods. There were baskets of fish, fruit and vegetable stands, bread, fabric, and butcher stalls. Oliver slowly stepped off the cart. He thanked the farmer before wandering out into the crowd.

It was quite dangerous for Oliver at first. He was so caught up in his surroundings that he did not pay attention to where he was walking. He had barely gone ten feet before a strange man pulled him from the path of a cart. "Watch where you're going, boy!" he said. "You're going to lose your head."

Oliver tipped his hat to the man to say thanks. He tried to be more careful, but it was hard. There was so much to look at! He decided it would be best if he sat on the curb for a while. He would have plenty of time to watch without getting hurt. After several minutes of staring into the street, he realized that someone was staring right back at him.

It was a strange looking boy not much older than Oliver. However, he was dressed very differently. His clothes were much too big for his small body. Even his hat was far too large. The suit jacket must have belonged to a gentleman at one time but was now ragged and worn. The boy was not bothered by his tattered hand-me-downs, though. He seemed quite confident and sure of himself. He stuck his thumbs in the vest pockets and walked across the street toward Oliver.

"Hello there! What's the row?" the strange boy asked.

Oliver looked behind him wondering who this boy was addressing. The boy must be talking to someone else. Oliver did not even understand the question.

"Hey," the boy said. He put his hand on Oliver's shoulder. "I asked how you are doing."

"Oh," Oliver replied. Now, that was a question he understood. "Fine, thank you. Well, I am very tired and hungry." Tears were forming in Oliver's eyes but he fought them back. He did not want to cry in front of this new boy. After all, this was the only person he knew in the city. "I've been walking for five days," he added.

"Five days!" the boy said. "Whatever for? Are you running from the law?" Oliver looked confused. Why ever would the law be chasing him?

"Ah, never mind," the boy said. "Makes no difference to me." He stuck his hand out. "Pleasure to meet you. My name's Jack Dawkins, but everyone calls me the Artful Dodger. Dodger for short."

Oliver stood up to shake his hand. "It's a pleasure to meet you, too. My name is Oliver Twist. I've come to London to make my fortune!"

Dodger raised his eyebrows. "You have, have you?" Dodger seemed lost in thought. He circled Oliver a few times while repeating, "Well, well, well." At last he stopped and put his hands on the smaller boy's shoulders. "I would imagine that you're also in need of a place to stay tonight. Unless, of course, you already have friends or family in London."

"Oh, no," Oliver said quickly. "You're the only

soul I know here. I only arrived a few minutes ago."

Dodger smiled. He slapped Oliver on the back. "It just so happens that I know a nice old gentleman who might be of help. He's very good about letting young lads sleep at his home." Oliver's eyes lit up. "Of course," Dodger added. "He doesn't let just anyone stay with him." He watched a look of disappointment cross Oliver's face. "Luckily, though, I'm a special friend of his and I'm sure I can put in a good word for you."

"Oh, please do," Oliver exclaimed. "That would make me ever so happy."

"Then it's all settled," Dodger said. He put his hands on his hips. He looked very pleased with himself. "We can't head over there just yet. We'll have to wait until dark."

"Whatever for?" Oliver asked.

"This gentleman," Dodger said slowly. "He's

very busy during the day. We can't just go by anytime."

Oliver thought this made sense. He followed Dodger through the market and into the backstreets of London. He told his new friend about his life at the workhouse and the undertaker's. Dodger listened to his stories but seemed distracted. Every once in a while, Dodger disappeared. He returned a few moments later with bread, cheese, or some fruit. Oliver did not see him pay for any of these items. He assumed Dodger knew the storekeepers. As day turned into night, Dodger pulled Oliver into darker and narrower streets. Without being told, Oliver understood they were on their way to the old gentleman's house.

CHAPTER 9

At Fagin's House

Oliver followed Dodger down dark and muddy London streets. All of the buildings they passed looked abandoned, although Oliver noticed candlelight in a few. For a moment, Oliver wondered if it was a good idea to follow this strange boy. Finally, Dodger stopped in front of an old rundown building. There was no glass in the windows and the stairs looked about to fall down.

Dodger pulled Oliver into the hallway and quickly closed the door. He whistled softly toward the end of the hall. A strange voice replied, "Hey now!"

"It's Dodger and a new friend. We're coming in." Dodger walked down the hall and up the flight of stairs. Oliver, still clutching his bag, followed. He stepped carefully along the hallway. A boy sat at the top of the stairs. He was dirty and wearing clothes far too small for him. He looked Oliver in the eye but did not smile.

"Is Fagin upstairs?" Dodger asked him. The boy nodded. Dodger and Oliver walked up to the next floor.

They entered a large, messy room. Soot covered the walls and old blankets covered the open windows. Several boys lay around on piles of sacks that served as beds. Other boys were sitting around a table playing cards. An old man in a torn trench coat stood in the corner. He wore a wide-brimmed black hat and had a long red beard. He was cooking sausages with one hand and straightening laundry with the other. Several dozen handkerchiefs were drying on a clothesline near the fire. He turned to look at Dodger and Oliver as they entered.

"Now, now, now," he said. "Who has the Dodger brought to see us?

"Fagin," Dodger said. "May I introduce my new friend Oliver Twist." Dodger took off his hat and bowed toward Fagin, then Oliver. The boys at the table laughed as Oliver bowed in return.

Fagin shoved one of the boys. "Charley Bates, be quiet! You don't know a gentleman when you see one." He turned to Oliver and performed a low, long bow. "It's an honor to meet you, Oliver Twist. Welcome to our home."

"Thank you so much for letting me stay, sir," Oliver said. "It's been days since I slept in a real bed."

"And I'm sure it's been just as long since you had a real meal." Fagin smiled.

"Longer than you can imagine," Oliver replied.

"Boys!" Fagin called. "Make room at the table for our new guest. Oliver will have our finest sausages tonight!" Charley and the other boys cleared a spot. They watched with envy as Fagin placed four large sausages on Oliver's plate.

"Eat up my dear boy," Fagin said. While Oliver enjoyed his supper, Fagin pulled Dodger and Charley aside. The three had a long whispered conversation. They came back to the table when Oliver was done. Fagin told the rest of the boys to get their supper. They all rushed to the fire and fought over the remaining meat.

"Oliver, my boy," Fagin said as he sat down, "Dodger here tells me you're out to seek your fortune. Do you have any idea what you might do?"

"No, sir," Oliver said. "Do you have any suggestions? I'm happy to try anything."

"Very positive thinking," Dodger said. He slapped Oliver on the back. Charley burst out laughing. He stopped when Fagin kicked his leg under the table.

"I'm sure that you could start by helping out around here," Fagin said. "We have many projects on the go."

"Are you a laundry, sir?" Oliver asked.

"A laundry?" Fagin was surprised by the boy's question. "Why would you think we're a . . . A-ha," he said. "You must be asking about our silk handkerchiefs drying by the fire." Oliver nodded. "We're in the business of, um, reselling used items."

The old man went to the clothesline and brought back a handkerchief for Oliver to examine. "Do you notice the fancy stitching Oliver? Very fine craftsmanship. Unfortunately, there are a few mistakes. We have to pick out the thread. That will be one of your jobs, Oliver. Would you like that?"

"Oh, yes, sir," he said. "That sounds wonderful."

Fagin smiled. He turned to Dodger and Charley and asked to see their work. "What have you boys picked up today?" Both boys handed the old man more handkerchiefs and two wallets.

"Oh, lovely work gentlemen," Fagin said. He rubbed the leather wallets. He saw that Oliver was looking at him. "What do you think, Oliver? Haven't Dodger and Charley done a wonderful job with these wallets?" He opened one up and examined the contents. "My, my," he said. "Very nice lining, my boys. Very nice indeed."

"Did they make them, sir?" Oliver asked. Oliver did not notice as Fagin removed several pound notes and put them in his pocket.

Once again Charley burst out laughing and Fagin silenced him with a shove. "You'll learn how to do the same soon enough, my boy. I'm sure that you'll soon be my star student."

Oliver was not sure what to make of Fagin and these boys. It seemed like a very strange family.

But Oliver knew he was in no position to judge. He had never known a family. He did not know if this was right or wrong. He did know that his belly was finally full. He had a bed to sleep in and people to watch over him in the morning.

CHAPTER 10

A New Game

It was late in the morning when Oliver woke up from a long, restful sleep. The room was empty except for Fagin. He was making coffee while softly whistling to himself. Oliver did not get up. He heard his name being whispered, but he did not respond. Oliver stayed in his bed, listening to the sounds of the city and watching the old man with half-closed eyes.

Fagin reached above the fireplace. He moved some bricks aside and slowly pulled a small box out. Oliver watched Fagin rub the top of the box, then lift the lid. One by one the old man removed the contents. One jewel after another, one gold watch after another. All of them sparkled and shone in the sunlight. Fagin turned them around and looked at them lovingly. He was lost in this activity for several minutes before noticing Oliver. The boy was watching from his bed.

The old man slammed the box shut, shoved it back in its hiding place, and jumped toward Oliver. He grabbed the boy by the shirt collar and pulled him up. "What did you see, boy? What did you see?" He was very angry and Oliver was terrified.

"N-n-nothing, sir! I swear," Oliver stuttered. "I just saw a few pretty things is all. I didn't mean to disturb you." Oliver did not understand why Fagin was so angry. He was not even sure what he had seen.

Fagin saw that Oliver meant no harm. "I'm sorry, boy. I was only trying to frighten you. You should be careful about who you watch around here. Not everyone is as trusting and forgiving as I am." He let go of Oliver's collar. The boy sank back down into his bed.

"Did you see any of the pretty things, my boy?" Fagin asked. He spoke gently again. Oliver nodded. "Well," Fagin said. "Those pretty things are for my retirement. Something to help me through my old age."

"That's very wise, sir," said Oliver. "I'm sure it costs a lot to help so many boys like Dodger and Charley. It must be difficult to save."

"Yes, my dear." Fagin smiled. "One must plan ahead." He rubbed Oliver's head. "And now it's time to get up. There are still a few sausages from breakfast."

Oliver stood up. He changed into another shirt and sat at the table. Even with sunlight coming through the open windows the room still looked dismal. As a matter of fact, the sunlight only made the dirt and grime easier to see. Oliver finished his meal and asked Fagin what he could do to help.

"How would you like to play a game?" Fagin said.

This was something new for Oliver. There had been very few chances in his life to play games. By the time he and the other boys had finished their day at the workhouse, they were too tired to play. "What sort of game would you like to play?" he asked.

"It's quite simple," Fagin replied. He filled his pockets with various items: a small box, a watch, a wallet, and a handkerchief. "Now," he said. "I want you to try to remove these objects from my pockets without me noticing."

Oliver giggled. "How will I do that?"

"Simply try, my good boy," Fagin said. "Wait until I'm looking the other way and carefully reach in."

Fagin slowly walked around the room. He pretended to look out the window or closely examine a book or glass. Oliver snuck up beside him and tried to pull out the wallet. Fagin turned suddenly and Oliver jumped back. He continued walking about the room without comment. The boy tried again and was successful the second time. He held the wallet up for Fagin to see, but the old man ignored him. Oliver understood that he should try for the other objects.

Finally Fagin said, "You're a clever lad, my dear. One of the smartest I've ever seen. If you go on this way, you'll be the greatest man of the time." Oliver wondered how taking things from Fagin's pockets would make him a "great man."

At that moment, the door flew open and two women walked in. "Well, Fagin," one of them said. "What do you have to say today?"

"Nancy," the old man said. "You startled me. You shouldn't surprise an old man like that."

"Ah," Nancy replied. "It'll take a lot more than a scare to put an end to you." She noticed the young boy holding the wallet and handkerchief. "What now," she said. "Who's this?"

Oliver looked at Nancy. She was the most beautiful woman he had ever seen. She was in her early twenties with long red hair. Her dress was stained and had worn edges, but Oliver did not notice. Nancy's bright green eyes watched him closely. She nudged her friend, a smaller dark-haired girl.

"Well, come now Oliver," Fagin said. "Say hello to Nancy and Bet."

Oliver bowed toward the women. They bowed in return.

"It's nice to finally meet a proper gentleman, Oliver," Nancy laughed. "Wouldn't you agree, Bet?"

"Certainly," Bet said. "He's like a breath of

fresh air." The two women laughed. It was not mean, though. Nancy and Bet had lived hard lives, but they still had kind hearts. They did not show a soft side often, but Oliver brought it out in them.

The young boy blushed from all the attention. He looked at the old man. Fagin was laughing to himself, clearly pleased with the events.

Nancy placed her basket on the table and held her hand toward Fagin. "I've come for Bill's money. He sent me round for it." Nancy stopped smiling.

Oliver watched as Nancy and Fagin argued over the money owed. This was the first time our young hero heard the name Bill Sikes. He quickly understood that Bill was Nancy's boyfriend and that Fagin owed Bill money. Oliver noticed something unusual in Fagin's voice. The old man seemed nervous while discussing Bill. Oliver eventually realized that everyone was afraid of Bill Sikes.

When Nancy got the money—all the money she asked for—she picked up her basket. "Are you ready, Bet?" she said. "It's time we were off." Oliver followed them to the door.

"And you, my fine young man," Nancy said. She held his chin in her hand. "You had best take care of yourself. And don't let this old man change you too much." Nancy kissed him on one cheek and Bet on the other.

Oliver blushed again. He waved at the two women as they walked out the door.

CHAPTER 11

Pickpockets

Oliver stayed in Fagin's room for several days. He enjoyed himself at first. He kept busy picking initials and thread out of handkerchiefs. He played the pickpocket game with the old man. He listened to the stories the other boys told when they returned in the evening. Nancy often stopped by, too. She was usually on an errand for Bill, but sometimes it was a friendly visit. "Just wanted to see my little gentleman," she would say. Oliver almost always blushed as she ruffled his hair.

One time Bill Sikes came on his own. All the boys stopped talking as soon as he walked in. Bill was a big man. His coat was tight over his large chest and arms. He had a wide firm jaw and dark cold eyes. He had a small dog named Bull's Eye, who followed him everywhere. The dog was short and squat and just as tough as his master. Bill did not speak as he moved across the room. Only Dodger was brave enough to nod as Bill walked past. Oliver realized it was best to stay out of his way. The boy kept to his corner bed until Bill left.

After a week or so, Oliver was bored with this routine. He wanted to go out with the other boys. He was excited to see more of London.

"Come on, Fagin," Dodger urged. "Let us take young Oliver out. He's ready by now. Don't worry, Charley and I will take care of him."

"Oh, yes please, sir," Oliver begged. "Please let me go out with Dodger and Charley."

The old man thought about it for a few moments. "All right," he said. "But be careful! You're in charge, Dodger," Fagin spoke sternly. "You watch out for Oliver."

Dodger saluted Fagin with his cap. "Right-o!" he said. He pulled Oliver's sleeve and they raced out the door. Charley followed quickly behind.

The two boys took Oliver to a new part of the city. There were no empty and rundown buildings on these streets. The sidewalks were clean, the buggies were shiny, and all of the people were well dressed. All of the people except Oliver, Dodger, and Charley, of course. There were so many people on the street that no one noticed them.

Oliver walked behind his friends. He watched as they picked their way through the crowd. Dodger would stand very close to a gentleman while Charley kept watch. When Charley gave a quick, sharp whistle, Dodger jumped back and they walked away. This happened several times as Oliver watched. He was confused about this game. What exactly were they doing?

Dodger pointed toward a gentleman at a book store. The older man was leaning over a table of books in the front of the store. "He'll do," said Dodger.

"A perfect target," Charley said. He took his usual post a foot or two away from Dodger and the well-dressed gentleman.

Dodger lifted the flap of the gentleman's jacket and removed his wallet. The man continued to look through the book table. This all happened in the space of a second or two. Dodger and Charley quickly ran back into the crowd.

Oliver was horrified! He stood a few feet away from the gentleman, shaking. He suddenly realized the "game" that Fagin was teaching him. These boys were all pickpockets and thieves. Fagin wanted Oliver to learn how to steal. The poor boy had no idea what to do next. He was frozen to his spot on the sidewalk. Oliver watched in terror as the gentleman reached for his wallet and found an empty pocket. He turned around quickly and saw Oliver standing a few feet away!

"Thief!" the man yelled. He pointed at Oliver. "Stop that boy! He stole my wallet!"

Oliver looked for Dodger and Charley, but he could not find them. He was so frightened that he started to run. A crowd followed him shouting, "Stop, thief!" If Oliver had looked behind him he might have seen his two friends in the crowd. They could not think of a better place to hide than in a crowd of good citizens.

Oliver ran down several streets. The crowd continued to grow and Oliver became more nervous. His legs grew weak with fear. Sweat and tears were filling his eyes, making it difficult to see. He tried to jump over some crates, but he tripped and landed hard on the sidewalk. He cut his knee, elbow, and forehead. Members of the crowd quickly grabbed him and pulled him up.

"Where's the gentleman that was robbed?" one of the men asked.

"He's coming through right now," a woman answered.

Mr. Brownlow, for that was the old gentleman's name, made his way through the crowd. He stopped when he saw Oliver. Something about the boy touched the old gentleman's heart. The boy was so small and clearly scared. Mr. Brownlow saw that Oliver was hurt. He felt pity for the boy, but a crime had been committed. Justice must be served.

"Is this the boy who stole your wallet?"

"I'm afraid so," said Mr. Brownlow. "Poor fellow. He has hurt himself."

The men in the crowd laughed at Mr. Brownlow's concern. They flagged down a police officer. Arrangements were made to take Oliver to court right away. The crowd set off for the courthouse, dragging the young boy behind them.

"Please be careful," Mr. Brownlow said. "Try not to injure him more." The old gentleman followed along. There was something about this boy—and this robbery—that did not sit well with him. Mr. Brownlow was certain there was more to this story.

CHAPTER 12

At the Courthouse

Dodger and Charley ran straight back to Fagin. They told the old man of Oliver's arrest. "They grabbed him right in the street," Dodger said. "There was nothing we could do."

Fagin was furious. He jumped up and yelled at the boys. "Why weren't you watching him? Do you know what this means?" Fagin pounded his fist on the table. "What if he talks to the police? What if he tells them where we live?"

Dodger and Charley tried to make excuses but Fagin would not listen. "Dodger!" he yelled. "Get to the courthouse right now. Come back and report everything that is said."

"Right-o, Fagin," Dodger said. "I won't let you down." Dodger raced out the door.

The courthouse was packed with people. Dodger found a seat in the back and waited for Oliver's turn before the judge. He noticed Mr. Brownlow seated a few rows ahead. Dodger sank down in his chair hoping that the old gentleman would not recognize him.

Finally Oliver was brought out. He was very pale and looked ready to faint. The guard put him in the prisoner's box. Oliver was so small that the judge could not see him over the railing.

"Give the prisoner a crate to stand on," the judge yelled. The entire courtroom was buzzing with excitement. Many members of the crowd that chased Oliver were there to see his sentencing. They weren't used to adventures in the middle of the afternoon. "How can anyone expect me to work in these conditions?" the judge said. He was often confused by his hectic courtroom. It put him in a very foul mood. He had a very short attention span and paid little mind to detail. Needless to say, the judge was not very good at his job.

"What's your name?" the judge asked Oliver.

Oliver tried to speak but he was too scared. He was still dizzy from his fall on the sidewalk. There were so many people around him and everyone seemed to be shouting. He whispered his name to the guard.

"Oliver Twist," said the guard.

"Oliver what?" the judge asked. "Did you say 'Twist'? What kind of name is Twist?"

The guard read out the charges against Oliver. He pointed to Mr. Brownlow, saying that he was the victim of the robbery. Oliver looked up from the prisoner's box and whispered for a drink of water.

"Don't be silly," the judge said. "Do you think this is a restaurant?"

The guard looked at Oliver. "Sir, I think the boy might really be ill," he said. "I could quickly grab him a drink."

"Nonsense! My day is too busy for such delays." The judge pounded his gavel on the desk. "Does the victim have anything to say?"

Mr. Brownlow stood up. He looked to Oliver, wishing he could help. "Only that I think the boy should be given water. Whether or not he's a thief, he's still a young boy."

The judge pounded his gavel again. "I've already given my answer regarding the water. Let's move along."

Oliver heard very little of this conversation. He was becoming light-headed. The room started to spin around him. Finally he collapsed, falling off the crate and onto the floor of the prisoner's box. The guard rushed to help him.

"Enough of this," said the judge. "The prisoner is sentenced to three months of hard labor. Guard, take him away."

"I won't allow it," shouted Mr. Brownlow. "This boy is ill. He needs a doctor, not a jail sentence."

"If you speak against me one more time," the judge said to Mr. Brownlow, "you'll receive a sentence of your own."

The door to the courtroom suddenly flew open. The owner of the bookstore where Mr. Brownlow was shopping came in. He rushed to the front of the room.

"This boy is innocent," he exclaimed. "I saw the whole thing from inside my shop. It was two other boys who stole the wallet. This boy was only standing nearby."

"But I've already sentenced the Twist boy," the judge whined. "Why didn't you come sooner?"

"I needed someone to watch my shop," the

bookseller said. "I only got away a few minutes ago."

The guard opened up the prisoner's box and picked up Oliver. He felt the boy's forehead. Oliver was burning up with a fever.

"Please bring the boy to my carriage outside," Mr. Brownlow said. "I'll take him back to my house. It's the least I can do."

No one noticed a boy running behind Mr. Brownlow's carriage as it made its way slowly down the street. Dodger had snuck out of the courtroom—careful to avoid the eye of the bookseller—and was now following Oliver and Mr. Brownlow home.

CHAPTER 13

A Safe Place

Oliver woke up in a very different room. He had never seen a place like it before. He was lying in a big comfortable bed. There were heavy warm blankets and many pillows. Fresh flowers sat on a side table. Clean curtains covered the windows, blocking out the morning sun. Oliver wondered if he was dreaming.

The door opened and an old woman walked in. She was carrying a breakfast tray. "Oh, thank heavens," she said when she saw Oliver. "At long last you are awake."

She put the tray down on the bedside table. "My name is Mrs. Bedwin. I'm Mr. Brownlow's housekeeper. I was watching over you while you were asleep with a fever."

"Good morning," Oliver said. He was surprised that he could speak. He realized at that moment that he was not frightened. For the first time in a very long time he was not afraid. "My name is Oliver Twist."

"Oh, yes, Oliver," Mrs. Bedwin smiled. "We know your name. Unfortunately, that is the only thing we know about you."

Mrs. Bedwin opened the curtains to let the morning sun in. "I've brought you some broth. I want you to eat it all up so you'll get your strength back. Then we can bring you a proper meal." She helped Oliver sit up in bed.

"I'm sorry, Mrs. Bedwin," Oliver said. "But could you please tell me where I am. Is this heaven?"

"On my word," Mrs. Bedwin gently scolded. "You should not say such things." She sat on the side of Oliver's bed. "I guess you don't remember anything past the courthouse, do you?"

Oliver shook his head.

"Mr. Brownlow, the man who lost his wallet, brought you home when you fainted," she said. "He's a very kind gentleman. He wanted you to have the best care."

"It's very kind of him, indeed," said Oliver. He thought he might cry again.

"Mr. Brownlow is very generous. Perhaps he'll come see you this afternoon if you feel better." Mrs. Bedwin got up to leave. "Now, can you handle this soup on your own, or should I help?"

"I'll be fine." Oliver smiled. "Thank you, Mrs. Bedwin. And I would like to meet Mr. Brownlow. I owe him many thanks."

Mrs. Bedwin leaned over and kissed Oliver's forehead. Oliver felt overwhelmed by this gesture of kindness. He could not hold back the tears. This time, however, they were tears of joy.

~

Meanwhile, in a more remote part of the city, Fagin was meeting with Dodger, Nancy, and Bill Sikes. They sat at the long table in Fagin's room. Their mood was very serious.

"Why should any of this worry me?" asked Bill. "If the boy turns you in it's no concern of mine." He looked at Fagin.

"You should make it a concern," Fagin warned. "If the police take me then it only seems likely that you'll be next." Bill reached across the table for Fagin's neck. The old man moved away just in time. "Now, Bill," Fagin said. "You really must watch your temper."

"All right, old man," Bill sat. He sat back in his

chair and crossed his arms. "What do you have in mind?"

"Why can't you leave the boy alone?" Nancy insisted. "Why do you want to drag him down to our level?" She was determined to save Oliver from a life of crime. Nancy knew this was not going to be easy. She had never spoken out against them before. There had never been a reason before Oliver.

"Keep quiet, girl!" Bill yelled. "You'll do what we tell you to do!" Bull's Eye sat beside his master and growled. Whenever Bill growled, so did the dog.

"Bill's right," Fagin said more gently. "We all have to stick together right now." Fagin tried to look as innocent as possible. "I think that someone more trustworthy should watch for him in the streets. At the first opportunity he—or she—could grab him." Fagin looked toward Nancy as he spoke.

"No." She shook her head. "No, and no, and a thousand times no. I won't do it!"

"She'll do it, Fagin," Bill said.

"No, she won't, Fagin!" Nancy replied.

"Oh, yes, she will, Fagin," Bill took hold of her arm and squeezed it. "And there'll be no more arguing."

Nancy winced but tried not to show how much her arm hurt. She held her head high. "You know I'd never hurt you, Bill. Please don't ask me to do this."

Bill looked at the old man. "She'll do it, Fagin," he said again.

CHAPTER 14

The Painting

Oliver was happy for the first time. His life with Mr. Brownlow was wonderful. He and the old gentleman often sat together in the study reading. Mr. Brownlow even helped Oliver learn his multiplication tables. "We'll send you to school in the fall, Oliver," he said. "Just as soon as you are ready."

"I'd like that very much, sir," Oliver said. "There wasn't much time in the workhouse for school. I can read a bit because some of the older boys taught me."

Mr. Brownlow and Mrs. Bedwin were very fond of Oliver. The boy was a wonderful addition to their household. Mr. Brownlow thought there was something familiar about Oliver. He was certain that Oliver reminded him of someone.

One afternoon, Mr. Brownlow pointed to a painting above the fireplace. "Tell me something, Oliver," he said. "Does the woman in the painting look familiar to you?"

"I've noticed that before, sir," Oliver replied. He stood before the painting and examined it closely. "It's funny, but she looks a bit like me." He looked to Mr. Brownlow. "She is very pretty, though. Who is she?" he asked.

Mr. Brownlow looked sad. "It's a very long story, I'm afraid, and not a very happy one." He put a hand on Oliver's shoulder. They both looked up at the painting. "A very good friend of mine gave me the painting shortly before he died. It's a picture of a young woman he loved very much."

"What happened to her?" Oliver asked.

Mr. Brownlow looked down at Oliver. He ruffled the boy's hair. "I'm afraid I don't know, Oliver. I don't even know her name."

Mrs. Bedwin came into the room with a package. "The bookseller dropped off your order, Mr. Brownlow. Shall I put it on your desk?"

"Oh, I have some books to return," Mr. Brownlow said. "Has he already left?"

"I'm afraid so," Mrs. Bedwin said.

"That's a shame," Mr. Brownlow said. He sounded disappointed.

"Let me return them," Oliver said. He was excited to be of some service to Mr. Brownlow. "You've been so kind to me," he said. "Please let me run this errand for you."

Mr. Brownlow was not convinced. "Are you sure you're feeling well enough? Do you know the way to the bookstore?" he asked.

"I feel fine, sir," Oliver said. "As good as I ever have. I won't get lost, either. I swear."

"All right, then," Mr. Brownlow laughed. "You can run this errand for me."

Mr. Brownlow wrapped up the books with paper and string. He gave them to Oliver along with a five-pound note. "Pay my bill at the bookstore and bring me back the change," he said. Mr. Brownlow looked at the boy's sweet face. It was truly remarkable how much Oliver looked like the woman in the painting.

"I'll be back shortly," Oliver said brightly. As he ran out the front door he yelled, "Good-bye, Mr. Brownlow! Good-bye, Mrs. Bedwin!"

CHAPTER 15

Captured!

Oliver strolled happily down the street. He said hello to everyone he passed. He stopped to sniff flowers and look in store windows. "It's such a lovely day," Oliver thought to himself. It was hard to believe that he left the workhouse a few months before.

As Oliver walked through the busy marketplace, he heard someone call his name. "Why if it isn't Oliver!" It took the boy several seconds to recognize Nancy. He did not expect to see her in that part of the city. She crossed the street to give him a hug.

"It's so good to see you!" she exclaimed. "Wherever have you been?"

Oliver was glad to see Nancy, too. She had always been so kind to him. "What are you doing here?" he asked. "It's funny seeing you in this neighborhood."

Nancy looked over her shoulder. She signaled to someone across the street. She turned back to Oliver with a grin, but she did not look happy. Oliver wondered if anything was wrong.

"I was just passing by and happened to see you," she said. "I sometimes do business in this part of town, you know." Nancy took Oliver's hand. "Why don't we stop for a cup of tea and catch up? I'd love to hear your news."

"I'm sorry, Nancy," Oliver said. "I can't do that right now. I have to run an errand for

Mr. Brownlow." The young boy sounded very serious.

"I won't keep you long." Nancy laughed nervously. She looked over her shoulder again. "Why don't we walk together for a while then." She held Oliver's hand and led him across the street.

Oliver started to tell Nancy all about Mr. Brownlow. He described the beautiful house and his warm bed. Nancy listened quietly. Oliver did not notice how pale she was or that her hands trembled. "I know a shortcut," said Nancy. She led him down an alleyway. Bill Sikes was standing in the shadows waiting for them.

Bill grabbed Oliver. He put his hand over the boy's mouth so Oliver could not scream. Oliver struggled to free himself, but the man was far too strong. A wagon was waiting for them. Bill got in the back with Oliver and hid beneath some blankets. Nancy sat up front with Dodger. Bill gave the signal and Dodger urged the horses to move.

The wagon made its way back to Fagin's place with Bull's Eye running behind. Oliver had no idea what might happen to him. He worried that he might be hurt. He worried that he would get in trouble with the police. Most of all, though, he worried that Mr. Brownlow might think he ran off with the money. Oliver's eyes teared up at the thought of disappointing Mr. Brownlow.

CHAPTER 16

Monks

A few days later, Bill Sikes walked into Fagin's room carrying a large bag. He dropped it on the table with a loud bang. "Get the boy ready," he growled. "He's coming with me on a job."

"Bill," Fagin protested. "Do you think that's a good idea? We just got the boy back." Fagin looked over at the boy. Oliver was huddled in the corner on one of the beds. Nancy sat with him. She had her arms wrapped around him.

Someone new was sitting in the room. He

wore a long black coat and a scarf that went up to his chin. He looked like a man in disguise. This strange new man sat silently in the corner across from Oliver. He paid no attention to Bill or Fagin as they spoke. Instead, he stared closely at Oliver. The boy felt uncomfortable under his gaze. "Who is that man?" Oliver whispered to Nancy.

She shrugged her shoulders. "His name is Monks. Fagin knows him. I see him every couple of months or so." Nancy looked at the man in the dark coat. "He gives me the creeps, though. He looks like he doesn't belong here." She paused for a moment. "Or like he's trying to hide something."

"I need someone small," Bill said to Fagin. "Oliver has to go through a window and let me into the house."

"He's too tired and scared, Bill," Nancy said. She tried to speak gently. "He's not up for it."

"Your opinions don't mean much around here," Bill said. He would not look at her. "Not anymore."

Nancy turned her face away. She was afraid tears might come. She had never cried in front of Bill or anyone. She did not want to start now. When she felt stronger she turned back to Bill.

"Take him then," she said. Her voice was now hard. She stood up from the bed.

"I don't need your permission, Nancy." His voice was calm but his eyes looked violent.

"All right, Bill," Fagin said quietly. "We don't want our friend Monks to think our little family doesn't get along." The old man nodded toward Monks, but the visitor did not notice. "Take Oliver if you need him. I'm sure you'll be more careful than Dodger and Charley."

Sikes dragged Oliver from his spot. He put his hand on the back of the boy's neck and led him to the door. Nancy took a step toward them, but stopped. Bill glanced at her as he passed by.

Oliver knew there was no point in fighting. He would have to do as the criminal asked. The boy did not cry as he set off with Bill.

CHAPTER 17

Breaking In

It was long after midnight by the time Bill and Oliver reached their target. It was a small but pretty house in a quiet part of the city. The house was surrounded by a great deal of land and trees. As a matter of fact, it looked more like a cottage than a house. Bill lifted Oliver over the small garden gate, then climbed over himself. He left Bull's Eye by the gate to watch for police.

Bill pointed toward a small round window near the back door. "That's the one, Oliver," Bill whispered. "See how it's already open a crack?"

The boy nodded. "You need to climb through. Then come around to the front and let me in."

Oliver nodded once more. He was afraid that he would make a mistake. He had often seen Bill angry, but had never seen him lose his temper. Oliver did not want to experience the rage of Bill Sikes.

"And be quiet about it, too." Bill pushed Oliver toward the house. "There's dogs in the kitchen. That's why I have to go in the front. Not as much noise."

Bill lifted the boy up. Oliver gently pushed the window open and climbed onto the sill. Although the window was very small, it was not as small as Oliver. He slipped inside easily. He stepped onto a table in the hallway then onto the floor.

He stood very still. There were no sounds in the house other than his own breathing. Oliver began to tremble. All of his limbs shook. He started to sweat. He considered running upstairs to wake up the owners. Oliver thought of Bill outside waiting for him. He realized he was too afraid of Bill to attempt an escape. So Oliver tiptoed toward the front door.

Bill was already there waiting for him. Oliver could see him through the mail slot. "Come on, boy," Bill barked at him. "Open up."

Oliver tried to unlock the door, but he could not pull the deadbolt. He tried and tried, but it would not budge. He used all his strength and the catch finally released. Unfortunately, Oliver also lost his balance and he tumbled across a table. A brass vase crashed to the floor. The boy jumped back in shock and terror.

Bill swung the newly unlocked door open. "What have you done?" he hissed. Bill saw the vase rattling down the hallway. He heard the dogs bark in the kitchen. "Come on, Oliver. We have to leave. Now!"

Oliver started backing away from Bill while shaking his head. This was his one chance to be saved. Someone else in the house had let the dogs out of the kitchen. The dogs started to race down the hall. Bill realized there was no hope with Oliver, so he turned and ran.

At first Oliver thought the dogs were coming to greet him. Then he recognized the sound of growls and snarls. The boy tried running toward the front door, but the dogs took hold of his pant leg. He was terrified. Oliver lost his balance once again. He fell to the floor, hitting his head on the hall table on his way down. Everything went black.

CHAPTER 18

The Locket

On the same night that Oliver and Bill broke into the house, Mr. Brownlow made an important discovery. The old gentleman had sent a letter to the workhouse looking for information about Oliver's past. He expected another letter in return, but he received two visitors instead.

Mr. and Mrs. Bumble arrived just after dinner. It was not often that the Bumbles visited a neighborhood or house as nice as Mr. Brownlow's. Both were dressed in their Sunday best, hoping to impress the gentleman. Mrs. Bedwin brought them into the study where Mr. Brownlow was reading the paper.

"Mr. Brownlow, sir," Mr. Bumble said. "We came from the workhouse when we heard you were looking for help." Mr. Bumble held his hat in both his hands. He was worried that his hands might start to shake.

Mr. Brownlow stood up to greet them. "So, you know Oliver Twist?" he asked.

"Know Oliver Twist?" Mr. Bumble said proudly. "I am the one who gave him that name! We've known him all his life."

Mrs. Bumble frowned at her husband's comments. "My husband means to say that we've been taking care of him all his life. Feeding him and giving him clothes. It's a thankless task, but we do it."

Mr. Brownlow saw right through Mrs. Bumble's remarks. He knew that she was not to be trusted. "And by feeding him do you mean serving watered-down gruel three times a day?" Mr. Brownlow asked. "Am I to understand that you consider dirty rags to be clothes? That forcing children to work all day in a bottle-washing factory is 'taking care of them'?" The old gentleman's voice was very harsh.

"I didn't come all this way to be insulted," Mrs. Bumble said rudely. "I could leave right this minute if I wanted."

"Of course you could," Mr. Brownlow said. "But I assume you have some information to sell or you wouldn't have come at all."

"Well," Mr. Bumble interrupted. He tried to sound friendly to lighten the mood. "We do have something for you. If you saw it fit to pay us for our trouble and expense, we'd be grateful, of course." Mr. Bumble smiled. He thought of himself as very wise, even though everyone else thought him a fool.

"Let me hear this news. Then we can discuss

payment," Mr. Brownlow replied.

Mr. Bumble nudged his wife. She removed a piece of cloth from her pocket. "We didn't even know this existed until few weeks ago," she said. "The old woman who was at Oliver's birth gave it to me just before she died." Mrs. Bumble unwrapped the cloth. She held up a gold locket and chain.

"Seems the boy's mother wanted Oliver to have this locket. It was the only thing she owned," Mrs. Bumble said. "The old woman decided to keep it for herself, though. I guess she felt guilty about it in the end. She wanted me to give it to Oliver, but he had run away by then."

"Then not long after," Mr. Bumble said, "we received a letter from you looking for information."

"That is very lucky, indeed," Mr. Brownlow said quietly. "May I?" He took the locket from

Mrs. Bumble. He slowly opened it up. Mr. Brownlow let out a long sigh when he saw the contents of the locket. He closed it again and shut his eyes.

Mrs. Bumble interrupted this moment of silence. "And you know, it wasn't easy getting here," she said. "It's hard to leave work. And there's the expense of the coach into London."

"You will be repaid for your troubles," Mr. Brownlow said. He called Mrs. Bedwin and asked her to see the Bumbles to the door. Mr. Brownlow gave them money to pay for the coach tickets and some extra as a reward. He was so distracted that he almost forgot to say thank you. The locket's contents shed new light on the Oliver Twist mystery. Mr. Brownlow could see the pieces coming together.

CHAPTER 19

Inside the Cottage

Bill Sikes! Oliver sat up quickly. Where was Bill Sikes? It was then that Oliver realized he was in yet another room. The wallpaper was decorated with tiny red roses. The windows were covered by white lace curtains. The boy's heart was pounding. Oliver realized that this place was safe. It had the same quiet calm of Mr. Brownlow's home.

Oliver walked to the window and lifted one of the lace curtains. He looked out into a beautiful garden. The yard was filled with lovely green trees and flowers in full bloom. He recognized the gate that Bill Sikes had lifted him over. The place looked so different in sunlight. It was not scary or dangerous at all.

A young woman was walking through the garden. She was picking flowers and placing them in a basket. She looked up and saw Oliver at the window. He was embarrassed about being discovered. She seemed quite happy to see him, though. She waved, then ran toward the house.

She opened the bedroom door a minute or two later. "Good morning," she said cheerfully. "I'm glad to see you're all right."

Oliver was surprised by her kindness. Did she not realize he had broken into her home last night?

"The doctor has already come and gone," she said. "He said the bump on your head wasn't serious. He thought you might be in a state of shock." She put her hand on his forehead to check for fever. Oliver stared at the young woman. She had a soft delicate face and light blond hair. She looked familiar to him, although he was certain they had never met before.

"Why don't you get dressed," she said. "You can come downstairs for some food." She pointed to a chair in the corner. "I left you some of Harry's old clothes. I'm afraid your pants were quite ripped up."

Oliver dressed slowly after she left. This was yet another strange turn in our young hero's life. He was once again saved from the hands of Fagin and Bill Sikes. He had once again woken up in a warm and comfortable bed. Oliver was quite sure that there was no way to know what the future might hold. He left the bedroom and, following the sound of soft voices, he made his way downstairs.

In the front room he found three people. Mrs. Maylie, the elderly owner of the house, sat by the fire knitting. Her son Harry, a young man about twenty-two years old, sat across from her. Rose, the young woman from the garden, stood by the window. She called Mrs. Maylie her aunt, but the two women were not related. Rose had lived with Mrs. Maylie since she was a very young girl. She was an orphan, just like Oliver. They stopped talking as Oliver walked in.

Harry stood up. "Please have a seat," he said to Oliver. He pointed to a chair near the fire. "We have a lot to discuss." Oliver did as the young man asked.

"We should tell you right away that we've already spoken with the police," Harry said. Oliver looked to the floor. He felt very ashamed. "We gave a description of the man with you,"

Harry continued. "Our gardener saw him running away. The police, however, didn't recognize the description. We hope that you can provide more information."

Oliver nodded. "I will tell you all I know," he said. "I want nothing to do with them. I'm frightened that they will try to kidnap me again."

"Then you were with him under threat?" Rose asked. She turned to Mrs. Maylie and Harry. "I told you the boy was innocent!"

Harry smiled at Rose. "I should never have doubted your opinion," he said. Oliver quickly understood that Harry and Rose were in love.

"First of all, child," Mrs. Maylie said. "What is your name?" Mrs. Maylie had a kind and gentle voice. She had been a widow for many years. She was not a wealthy woman, but her family lived comfortably.

"Oliver Twist," he said.

"Now, Oliver Twist," Mrs. Maylie said as she put down her knitting, "please tell us how you came to be in our house in the dead of night."

So Oliver told them his whole history. He described his mother's untimely death, the workhouse, the undertaker's, his walk to London, and meeting Dodger, Fagin, Nancy, and Bill. He also told them about the strange man named Monks. It was a hard story to tell but Oliver spared no detail. He had lived among thieves and pickpockets and wanted no more of it. Oliver became quite upset when he described Mr. Brownlow. "He was very kind to me," the boy cried. "He must think that I've run off."

"Oh, you poor boy," Mrs. Maylie said. She was almost in tears. Harry put a hand on his mother's arm to comfort her.

Rose was very upset. As she spoke, her voice cracked. "And to think," she spoke through her tears, "that could have been me. If not for the kindness of my dear aunt, I might have been left to a life in a workhouse or among criminals."

Mrs. Maylie moved to her foster child's side. "Don't think about such things," she said softly. "We're lucky to have found each other." She kissed Rose's cheek. "And now Oliver is with us. I'm sure he was brought here for a reason."

Harry watched his mother and Rose. His face was as kind and concerned as Mrs. Maylie's.

"I'll head to the police station right now," Harry said. "Hopefully this information is enough to find this Bill Sikes and Fagin. Oliver," he said, "they may need to talk to you. Are you all right with that?"

"Yes, of course," Oliver said eagerly. "I'll help in any way I can."

Harry kissed his mother goodbye before leaving for the police station.

Oliver spent the rest of the day with Rose and Mrs. Maylie. He heard all about their lives. Many years ago, Mrs. Maylie and Harry had lived in a small city near the sea. When Harry was six years old, their minister came to see Mrs. Maylie. He had a young girl who needed a home. Her father had recently died and her older sister had disappeared. The church was looking for other members of the family, but they had very little information. They did not even know her last name. The little girl needed some place to stay while they searched. Mrs. Maylie said she was glad to help and took young Rose into her home.

"Did they not find any of your family?" Oliver asked. He felt sympathy for Rose. Oliver knew only too well the loneliness of an orphan.

"They found no one," she replied. "My father died without leaving any identification."

"Oh," Oliver said. "That is so sad."

"Don't feel sorry for me. I have been very lucky." Rose put her hand on the boy's arm. "My aunt, for that is what I call Mrs. Maylie, has given me a wonderful home. I have always been treated as family." Rose smiled at her foster aunt and then at Oliver.

"And we hope someday to make her even more a part of our little family," Mrs. Maylie smiled. "Our Harry has proposed marriage to Rose."

Rose looked to the floor. Her face flushed red. "I cannot accept, Aunt. You know my reasons." Mrs. Maylie tried to argue but Rose stopped her. "Harry will soon be a minister. It would be improper for him to marry a woman with an unknown past. It would create a scandal."

"Oh, Rose," Mrs. Maylie said sadly. The old woman knew there was no point in fighting. Rose's mind was set.

Oliver looked at these two kind women. He felt instant love for them. He wished there was something he could do to solve their problem. He would do anything to help, if only he knew how.

CHAPTER 20

A New Plan

Fagin and Bill were planning their next move. They knew it would not be as easy to snatch Oliver in the street again. Nancy was cooking sausages on the fire. She listened quietly to their conversation. Her face was very pale. She looked tired and worried.

The mysterious man named Monks once again sat in the corner of Fagin's room. This time, however, he was the one talking. His hat was pulled low over his face and his coat was buttoned high on his throat. The only recognizable part of him was a red scar across his left cheek.

"We must get Oliver Twist back," he hissed. "He is a danger to us all."

"Why do you care so much?" Bill asked. He was suspicious of this man. He had seen Monks in town a number of times, but they had not met until recently. Bill wondered why Monks tried to hide his identity. Everyone Bill knew was a criminal and everyone had a secret. There was something different about Monks, though. Monks was hiding something very unusual.

"It's none of your business why I care," Monks shot back. "I have information about Oliver Twist that I want to keep a secret. He cannot remain in that house—or with Brownlow. It will mean the end."

Fagin and Bill looked at each other. They both knew that they needed Monks. He had access to places and money that they did not.

Nancy placed a plate of sausages on the table in front of the men. "That's it for me," she said. She wrapped her shawl around her shoulders.

"Where do you think you're going?" Bill asked.

"I'm off to see Bet," Nancy said. She spoke with confidence, but her face was pale. Monks watched her while she spoke. "I'll be back in a couple of hours."

"Don't wander too far," Fagin warned. "We need to stick together right now."

"What's that supposed to mean, Fagin?" she snapped. "Haven't I always been here for you? Haven't I been stealing for you and cooking for you since I was a young girl?"

"Now, Nancy dear," the old man said. "Let's not get angry. We might suspect you have something to hide."

"How dare you!" she yelled.

"That's enough!" Bill said. "Go see Bet if you want. Just be home in two hours if you know what's good for you."

Nancy nodded. She touched Bill on the shoulder before running out the door.

A few minutes later Monks said a quick goodbye. He rapidly walked up the dark street in the same direction as Nancy.

CHAPTER 21

A Full Confession

After making a report at the police station, Harry went to visit Mr. Brownlow. Mrs. Bedwin brought him into the study. Harry quickly introduced himself.

"Mr. Brownlow, I know this may come as a surprise," Harry said. "But I've come with a message from Oliver Twist."

"Oliver?" Mr. Brownlow rose quickly from his chair. "You know Oliver? Where is he?"

"Don't worry," Harry said. "He's safe. At least for the time being. He was grabbed in the street by those bandits while running to the bookstore for you. A few days later a man named Bill Sikes forced him to break into my mother's home. Our dogs heard the intruders. Oliver was caught but Sikes escaped. My mother kept Oliver at her house during his recovery. We have grown very fond of the boy. He told us his sad story—including your kindness toward him. We want to help any way we can."

Mr. Brownlow sighed. "I am so relieved to hear that he is in safe hands. I was worried that he was in danger."

"So you knew all about Fagin, Sikes, and the young thieves?" Harry asked.

"No," Mr. Brownlow replied. "But I know of other dangers that threaten Oliver. I've been conducting my own investigation since he left. I already had my suspicions, but have since learned some very important details about our Oliver."

"My word!" Harry exclaimed. "May I ask what you have learned? I'm certain Oliver would want to hear all."

"I need to confirm a few more details before I say anything," Mr. Brownlow replied. "I hope you'll understand."

Harry nodded that he understood. "I really must be going," Harry said. "My mother and Rose will be expecting me."

Mr. Brownlow stood up to shake the young man's hand. "I cannot thank you enough for coming to see me," the old gentleman said. "Please give my love to Oliver. Let him know that I will come to see him very soon."

"Of course I will," said Harry. "He will be happy to hear you don't think him a thief."

"Never!" Mr. Brownlow exclaimed.

Harry Maylie was not gone ten minutes when there was another knock at Mr. Brownlow's door. This time, however, a young woman was admitted to his study. Nancy was very nervous. She kept her shawl wrapped tightly around her shoulders. She refused to sit down.

"I can't stay," she said quickly. "I've only come to warn you about Oliver."

"Whatever do you mean?" Mr. Brownlow said. "I've just had word that he is safe."

"For now," she said. "But there are plans to grab him again."

"How do you know all this?" Brownlow asked.

"Because I'm the one who nabbed him last time," Nancy blurted out. "I grabbed him while he was running to the bookstore. Please don't look at me like that," she exclaimed. "I know that I've done wrong. I've lived a bad life. I've been a thief since I was little. I know what it's like to live on the streets and I don't want that for Oliver." Nancy's eyes filled with tears.

"Come with me to the police," Mr. Brownlow said. "You could lead them to Fagin and his thieves."

"No!" Nancy exclaimed. "I won't go to the police. Never! I don't care what happens to me—or to Fagin for that matter—but there's one person that I must protect. If I go to the police they will want information about him. I won't do anything to hurt him."

"We can protect you if that's what you're worried about," Mr. Brownlow said. He was very concerned about this woman. He knew she was scared and that she was doing a very brave thing. "It's never too late to ask for forgiveness," he said.

"No." Nancy chuckled despite her tears. "It's too late for me."

"Then what are we to do?" Brownlow asked.

"They know where Oliver is staying," she said. "There's a strange man working with them.

He says that he knows the family well. He is determined to stop Oliver, but I don't know why. They plan to break into the house in the next day or so and grab Oliver." Nancy started to cry again. "Oh, Mr. Brownlow! I worry what they might do when they have him again. This strange man has me very worried."

"Do you know this man's name?" Brownlow asked. His voice was very calm.

"He calls himself Monks, but I don't know if that's his real name. He always wears a large hat and a coat buttoned to his neck. I suspect that he is hiding something."

"Can you tell me anything else about him?" Brownlow asked.

"Well," Nancy said slowly. She was thinking very carefully. "He has a red scar—a burn maybe—on his left cheek."

"Aha!" Brownlow exclaimed. "Just as I thought!"

"I'm sorry, sir," Nancy said. "Do you know him?"

"Alas," Mr. Brownlow said, "I know the man well."

Nancy looked very confused. It was a strange coincidence that Mr. Brownlow would know this man Monks. For the first time, Nancy wondered if there was something different about Oliver Twist.

"Will you be all right getting home?" Mr. Brownlow asked. "I would be happy to lend you my carriage."

She shook her head. "There's no need," she said. "I'm very comfortable in the streets at night. It's where I've spent much of my life."

Nancy said a quick good-bye then hurried out the front door. Mr. Brownlow watched her leave. He wished there was something more he could do to help her. If only he had looked out his front window to watch her walk down the street. He might have noticed a man dressed in a large hat and full coat following her. If only Mr. Brownlow had known what was about to happen.

CHAPTER 22

Off to Australia

"It was awful, Fagin," Charley wailed. "It was terrible watching Dodger in the prisoner's box." Charley sat at the table with Fagin and Bill. He had spent the day following Dodger through the courts and police station. Dodger had been arrested earlier that day for stealing a pocket watch.

"What did the judge say?" Fagin asked. "Come on boy, spit it out!"

"Take it easy, old man," Bill growled. "Having boys in the court isn't new. We've all been there before."

"This is Dodger, Bill!" Fagin cried. "He's my best and my brightest! If they get Dodger, what else could happen?"

"You're too superstitious old man," Bill laughed.

"Finish the story, Charley," Fagin pleaded. "Where is Dodger now? What did they give him?"

"They're sending him off," Charley said. "They're deporting him to Australia. He's leaving on the next ship out!"

"What?" Fagin jumped up from the table. "Dodger is off to Australia! This will never do!" he cried. "This is a disaster!"

The door to the room opened and Monks walked in. He sat in the chair between Fagin and Bill.

"It's a dark day," Fagin said to Monks. "Our Dodger has been nabbed. We've lost him."

"This boy should leave," Monks said pointing to Charley. "We need to have a talk." Fagin waved his hand and told Charley to leave the room.

When they were alone, Monks leaned in to Bill. "Would you like to hear where your girl Nancy went tonight?" he said.

Bill looked at this strange man. "What are you going on about?" he said. "She went off to see Bet."

"That's what she said but I happen to know the truth," Monks said.

Bill looked at Monks then Fagin. Fagin shrugged his shoulders to say he was just as confused.

"She went off to see Brownlow," Monks whispered in Bill's ear. "She told him everything to save that boy."

Bill stood up so quickly that he knocked his chair over. "You're a liar!" he yelled. "Nancy wouldn't do that. She wouldn't turn against me!"

"But she has Bill," Monks said. "I followed her. I know."

"Now, Bill," Fagin said. He tried to calm his friend down. "Don't do anything rash."

"Don't meddle where you don't belong, old man," Bill hissed. He pushed Fagin up against the wall. "This is my business. I'll take care of it." Bill turned on his heel and stormed toward the door. He knocked over chairs on his way out. Bull's Eye ran after his master.

"Bill!" Fagin yelled. He ran to the door and called to Bill down the stairs. "What are you going to do? What are you going to do?!"

CHAPTER 23

Nancy's Death

Bill wandered through the streets. People stepped aside as he passed. No one wanted to get in his way. No one wanted Bill's attention. His face was red with rage. His fists were clenched at his sides. He asked if anyone had seen Nancy. Everyone said no.

After an hour or so, Bill found her sitting on a doorstep. She stood up as soon as she saw him. Nancy started to back away. She saw the look in his eyes and she was afraid. "Bill, please," she said. "Why are you looking at me like that?"

Bill said nothing as he walked toward her. She backed her way around a corner as Bill followed her. A few moments later a terrible scream was heard. People standing in the street ran toward the sound. They turned the corner to see Bill Sikes running away from Nancy's lifeless body.

He called to Bull's Eye over his shoulder. "Come on," he snapped. "Bull's Eye! Come here!" The dog stood still. He stayed beside Nancy's body rather than follow his master. He turned away from Bill and sat down.

"Stop, murderer!" a man called. A few people ran after Bill. "Stop!" the man called again. "Someone get the police!" While some of the group stayed with Nancy's body, the rest ran after Bill.

Bill was panicked. He ran wildly through the streets. Every door he tried was locked. Every street and laneway was filled with people. Everyone was calling him a murderer. He heard his name echo through the streets and alleyways. Bill knew he had to hide. He needed money to get out of the city. He had to leave right away. He ran back to Fagin's with the crowd close behind.

All of Fagin's boys were back in the room preparing for bed. Bill ran in and grabbed Fagin by the collar. "I need money," Bill said. "Give me money so I can get away!"

Fagin spoke calmly. "Bill," he said. "You've got blood on your coat." He stepped slowly away from Bill. "What have you done?"

"I've saved us," Bill hissed. "She turned against us. I couldn't let her get away with it."

"No, Bill, no." Fagin shook his head. "This is not the way."

"Where's Nancy?" Charley called. He jumped from his bed and faced Bill. "What have you done with Nancy?"

Bill turned on the boy. "Don't cross me, Charley," he said. "I'm in a mood tonight."

They could hear the crowd approaching. Everyone in the room stopped to listen.

"You're a monster," Charley yelled at Bill. "A monster!" Bill took a step toward the boy. "Stay away from me!" Charley said. "All of you." He looked to everyone in the room. "I want nothing to do with any of you." Charley ran out of the building and joined the crowd out front. "He's upstairs," Charley told the policeman. "I can show you the way."

Bill knew his time was up. He grabbed some tools from the room, a few things he could sell, and a rope. He ran back into the stairwell and up to the roof.

He looked down at the crowd below. Its numbers had grown considerably. There was no way off the building except to jump to the next roof. He tied his bag of tools over his shoulder. Starting at one end of the roof, he ran toward the other and jumped across toward the next building.

Unfortunately, it was too far. He managed to grab a hold of the other side but his fingers slipped. Bill Sikes fell to his death as the crowd below screamed.

Meanwhile, Charley lead the police into the building. They caught Fagin on the stairs. He tried to avoid their grasp but they took hold and dragged him outside. Charley stayed right with them. "I'll tell you anything you need," he said to the police. "I've had enough of all these people."

CHAPTER 24

A New Family

Several weeks of quiet living passed. Life at Mrs. Maylie's seemed remarkably calm after so much excitement. It was a bright summer's day when Oliver was called in from the garden. Rose said that there was someone there to see him. Oliver jumped for joy when he saw Mr. Brownlow in the sitting room. He hugged the gentleman with all his might.

"Oliver," Mr. Brownlow said. "It's wonderful to see you. I'm glad to see you safe and in capable hands."

"It's wonderful here," Oliver said. "Everyone is kind and wonderful. It's just like living with you and Mrs. Bedwin."

Brownlow laughed and ruffled the boy's hair. "You're a lucky boy to have so many homes."

"Especially when I had none for so many years," Oliver replied.

"I've come with some very important news. I'm sure you will all want to hear it," Mr. Brownlow said. "First of all, I've heard from the police. Fagin has been sentenced to many years of hard labor. I think we can all relax on that front."

"It looks like you have nothing to worry about, Oliver," Harry said. He touched the young boy on the shoulder. "No Bill Sikes or Fagin to cause any more trouble. It is a shame about Nancy, though." Everyone in the room nodded sadly. Oliver looked like he might cry.

Mr. Brownlow took a deep breath. He asked

everyone to take a seat. "Now, would you please excuse me for a moment."

Brownlow walked into the hall. After a moment he returned with another man. It was none other than Monks! Oliver was horrified. He jumped from his seat and ran to stand beside Harry's seat.

"Don't worry, Oliver," Brownlow said. "Monks cannot hurt you now. As a matter of fact, he is here to help." Monks nodded slowly.

"My word," Mrs. Maylie said. "Whatever could this mean?"

"Oliver," Mr. Brownlow said. "Please come and sit by me. You are the center of this story. It has all come out because you were brave enough to come to London." Brownlow looked to Monks. "Shall I start the story?" Monks nodded once again but remained silent. He looked tired and ashamed.

"Do you remember the painting of the

woman above my fireplace?" Brownlow asked Oliver. The boy nodded.

"I noticed that painting, too," Harry piped up. "It was very striking."

"It was given to me by my oldest and dearest friend before he left on a long trip. He was going to Paris to settle his finances. His ex-wife and son lived there. My friend had fallen in love again and wanted to remarry. The painting is of Agnes, the young woman he loved. He asked me to keep it until he returned. Unfortunately, I received word several weeks later that my friend had died while abroad."

"Oh, how awful," Rose exclaimed. "I'm so sorry."

"Thank you, Rose," Mr. Brownlow said. "That's very kind of you." Brownlow took something from his pocket. "Now, Oliver. Would you be so kind as to look inside this locket?"

Oliver opened up the locket. He let out a gasp

when he saw the inside. "Mr. Brownlow!" he said. "It's the same woman from the painting!"

"Yes, my boy." Mr. Brownlow closed Oliver's hand around the locket. "This locket belongs to you."

"Me?" Oliver was taken aback. "Why would you give it to me?"

"It is your mother who wanted you to have it," Brownlow said. "She gave it to you shortly before she died, but greedy persons at the workhouse kept it from you. You see, Oliver, I noticed your similarity to the painting right away. I contacted Mr. and Mrs. Bumble at the workhouse seeking more information. They came to see me—looking for money, of course—and delivered this locket."

"My mother?" Oliver said. The boy was in shock.

"This is an amazing story," Rose exclaimed.

She hugged Oliver. "I'm so happy for you, Oliver. You've found your family."

"There's more to this story, Rose," Brownlow said. "And I think you'll find it of particular interest," he said to her.

"Me?" Rose said, sitting back down.

"I think it's time that we bring our guest into the story," Brownlow said. "Oliver, you know this gentleman by the name of Monks, but his name is actually Leeford. He is the son of my dear friend, Edwin Leeford."

"Then, does that mean...?" Mrs. Maylie spoke slowly.

"Yes," Monks said. "Oliver is my half-brother." He sighed and looked around the room. "My father arrived in Paris to discuss his will with my mother. He wanted to ensure that Agnes and their unborn child were taken care of in case anything happened. My father died before any papers were drawn up. Since my mother and I were still his legal heirs, we were the first to go through his belongings. We hid my father's wishes from the lawyers. We told no one about Agnes or the child. My mother was outraged. She did not want to part with any of my father's money. She was obsessed. And so was I."

"That's awful," Mrs. Maylie said. "How could she do such a thing?"

"I am just as guilty, madam," Monks said. "I was greedy and did not want to share my father's money. It didn't end there, though. We were both afraid of discovery. I'm afraid to say that I was nearly driven mad by this secrecy."

Everyone in the room sat quietly while Monks spoke. Oliver sat next to Rose on the couch. Her arm was draped over his shoulder.

"We knew enough about Agnes to track her down," Monks continued. "We discovered her father and younger sister living in the family home. Agnes had disappeared a few months earlier. I searched through the records of many towns and workhouses until I discovered the death of a young woman. She was Agnes's age and had given birth to a boy. The boy was still living in the workhouse. He had been given the name Oliver Twist. We worried that Agnes's family would make the same discovery. Her father, however, had grown sick with worry. He had moved to a seaside town with his young daughter and lived a life of isolation. He died in his small cottage, leaving the girl with no known relatives. My mother and I had hoped that all our problems were solved. The young girl was left with a widow. We assumed that she would be sent to an orphanage. The widow, however, considered her family and raised her as her niece."

Rose looked to

Mrs. Maylie, then Harry, then Mr. Brownlow. She was speechless.

"Am I to understand," Mrs. Maylie said, "that Rose was that girl?"

"Yes," Monks said. "I've been watching your family—from a distance, of course—for many years now. Rose is the younger sister of Agnes."

"I can't quite believe this," Rose said. Harry hugged her.

Oliver looked up at her. "That makes you my aunt."

Oliver hugged Rose once more. This time, however, he thought he might never let go.

"And that," Mr. Brownlow said, "is the end of the story." He ruffled Oliver's hair.

"That's funny," Harry laughed. "It feels like the beginning to me." He watched Rose and Oliver embrace. Rose smiled back at him.

"Oh, Mr. Brownlow," Mrs. Maylie said. "We

can't thank you enough! I think this means our Rose will finally agree to marry Harry."

The room was filled with laughter and tears. The only one who looked uncomfortable was Monks. He felt guilt and shame about his actions. Mr. Brownlow had agreed to not press charges. Monks agreed to give Oliver his share of the inheritance.

So, this is where we leave our young hero. Fear not, though: Oliver Twist lived a warm and happy life from that point on. Harry and Rose were married. Mrs. Maylie and Oliver continued to live with them in the sweet little house with the garden. Mr. Brownlow visited often. At long last, Oliver had a family. His life was filled with more people—and more love—than he ever could have imagined.

What Do *You* Think?

Questions for Discussion

Have you ever been around a toddler who keeps asking the question "Why?" Does your teacher call on you in class with questions from your homework? Do your parents ask you questions about your day at the dinner table? We are always surrounded by questions that need a specific response. But is it possible to have a question with no right answer?

The following questions are about the book you just read. But this is not a quiz! They are designed to help you look at the people, places, and events in the story from different angles. These questions do not have specific answers. Instead, they might make you think of the story in a completely new way.

Think carefully about each question and enjoy discovering more about this classic story.

1. How does Oliver compare to other boys you have read about? Which other character does Oliver remind you of the most?

2. In spite of his own needs, Oliver does his best to help Dick in any way he can. Why do you think he does this? Have you ever helped a friend even if it made your own situation worse? Do you have any friends that would do the same for you?

3. Do you believe Oliver was brave or desperate when he asked for more food? What would you have done in his position?

4. When Oliver leaves the workhouse to go live with the undertaker, he says that he hopes

it will be an adventure. Do you think it turns into the kind of adventure Oliver is looking for? What's the best adventure you've ever had?

5. When Oliver leaves the mortuary, he feels both frightened and excited. Have you ever had such mixed emotions?

6. Oliver seems to immediately trust every new person he meets. Why do you suppose this is? Have you ever trusted someone you shouldn't have?

7. After breaking into the Maylies' house, Oliver has a difficult choice to make: face their dogs or leave with Bill Sikes. What would you have done in his position? What is the most difficult choice you've ever had to make?

8. At one point in the story, Bill Sikes wonders what Monks is trying to hide. What did you think his secret was? Were you surprised to discover the truth? What is the biggest secret you've ever kept?

9. When Mr. Brownlow asks for information about Oliver, the Bumbles bring him a locket. Were you surprised at the contents of the locked? What did you expect it to contain?

10. By the end of the book, Oliver and Rose have both found their family. Do you think this is realistic? Have you ever known something like this to happen in real life?

Afterword

First impressions are important.

Whether we are meeting new people, going to new places, or picking up a book unknown to us, first impressions count for a lot. They can lead to warm, lasting memories or can make us shy away from any future encounters.

Can you recall your own first impressions and earliest memories of reading the classics?

Do you remember wading through pages and pages of text to prepare for an exam? Or were you the child who hid under the blanket to read with a flashlight, joining forces with Robin Hood to save Maid Marian? Do you remember only how long it took you to read a lengthy novel such as *Little Women*? Or did you become best friends with the March sisters?

Even for a gifted young reader, getting through long chapters with dense language can easily become overwhelming and can obscure the richness of the story and its characters. Reading an abridged, newly crafted version of a classic novel can be the gentle introduction a child needs to explore the characters and story line without the frustration of difficult vocabulary and complex themes.

Reading an abridged version of a classic novel gives the young reader a sense of independence and the satisfaction of finishing a "grown-up" book. And when a child is engaged with and inspired by a classic story, the tone is set for further exploration of the story's themes, characters, history, and details. As a child's reading skills advance, the desire to tackle the original, unabridged version of the story will naturally emerge.

If made accessible to young readers, these stories can become invaluable tools for understanding themselves in the context of their families and social environments. This is why the *Classic Starts* series includes questions that stimulate discussion regarding the impact and social relevance of the characters and stories today. These questions can foster lively conversations between children and their parents or teachers. When we look at the issues, values, and standards of past times in terms of how we live now, we can appreciate literature's classic tales in a very personal and engaging way.

Share your love of reading the classics with a young child, and introduce an imaginary world real enough to last a lifetime.

Dr. Arthur Pober, Ed.D.

Dr. Arthur Pober has spent more than twenty years in the fields of early-childhood and gifted education. He is the former principal of one of the world's oldest laboratory schools for gifted youngsters, Hunter College Elementary School, and former Director of Magnet Schools for the Gifted and Talented for more than 25,000 youngsters in New York City.

Dr. Pober is a recognized authority in the areas of media and child protection and is currently the U.S. representative to the European Institute for the Media and European Advertising Standards Alliance.

Explore these wonderful stories in our Classic Starts library.

20,000 Leagues Under the Sea

The Adventures of Huckleberry Finn

The Adventures of Robin Hood

The Adventures of Sherlock Holmes

The Adventures of Tom Sawyer

Anne of Green Gables

Black Beauty

Call of the Wild

Frankenstein

Gulliver's Travels

A Little Princess

Little Women

Oliver Twist

The Red Badge of Courage

Robinson Crusoe

The Secret Garden

The Story of King Arthur and His Knights

The Strange Case of Dr. Jekyll and Mr. Hyde

Treasure Island

White Fang